RAIL

GHOSTS

AND

HIGHWAY

HORRORS

RAILWAY GHOSTS AND HIGHWAY HORRORS

DANIEL COHEN

Interior illustrations by Stephen Marchesi

AN
APPLE
PAPERBACK

SCHOLASTIC INC.
New York Toronto London Auckland Sydney

ISBN 0-590-45423-4

Text copyright © 1991 by Daniel Cohen. Illustrations copyright © 1991 by Stephen Marchesi. All rights reserved. Published by Scholastic Inc., 730 Broadway, New York, NY 10003, by arrangement with Dutton's Children's Books, a division of Penguin Books USA Inc. APPLE PAPERBACKS is a registered trademark of Scholastic Inc.

12 11 10 9 8   4 5 6 7/9

Printed in the U.S.A.   28

First Scholastic printing, October 1992

FOR DONALD—

not a ghost but a free spirit

Contents

Introduction
Travelers' Tales

Tradition holds that ghosts wander about dusty castle corridors at midnight. Granted, a castle corridor at midnight is apt to be a pretty spooky place. But few of us are going to have the opportunity to wander alone through castle corridors, dusty or otherwise. If we ever do get into a castle, it is likely to be as part of a tour group in the middle of the afternoon. That is not an atmosphere which encourages meetings with ghosts.

Personally, I have always felt that one of the spookiest situations the average person is likely to encounter is to be driving along a deserted road at night, and in bad weather. There you are, isolated by your speeding automobile from all other human beings. You can only see what falls into the narrow beam illuminated by your headlights. Even then, you don't see things clearly. Objects and shapes flash by, and you're not quite sure what they were. Was that an oddly shaped tree by the side of the road? Or was a man standing there?

All around you there is the vast impenetrable darkness. Why anything—absolutely anything—might be out there. You feel very vulnerable. What if the car should suddenly break down? What would you do? How would you defend yourself from something that might come at you out of the darkness?

Tradition also holds that ghosts can be found most often at places where people have died violently. That's why castles, some of which have a long and bloody history, are considered prime territory for ghosts. But there are probably more violent deaths on the highways of America in a single year than there have been in all the castles in England in recorded history. If the ghosts of those who died by violence haunt the places where they died, then the highways could be lined with the spirits of accident victims. And to hear some people talk, they are.

Highways and roads are the setting for many of the most widely known, and widely believed, ghostly accounts today. There are hitchhiking ghosts, and ghosts who pick up hitchhikers. There are ghost cars, trucks, and motorcycles. There are phantom dogs, and even stranger supernatural creatures that have been reported by frightened drivers. There are ghosts that help, ghosts that hurt, and ghosts that just seem to hang around.

In short, there are more surprises in driving than you ever imagined.

Railroads are also the scene of more than their share of ghost accounts. The railroad has remained a more important means of transportation in Great Britain than it is in the United States. For that reason, most, though not all, of the railroad ghosts in this book are British.

Are the stories in this book true? Did they actually happen? I didn't make them up, though somebody might have. I have heard them and enjoyed them, and that's what you should do, just enjoy them. And the next time you find yourself in a car on a dark and deserted road, you may ask yourself, "I wonder what's really out there?" And you may find yourself answering, "I don't really want to know."

1

The Most Famous Phantom

Late on a rainy, dreary Saturday evening in November, Jim Hamelton found himself driving down a deserted road north of Chicago. He was returning from a business trip that had been much longer than he had expected, and he was exhausted. It was an effort just to keep his eyes open and on the road.

Then his headlights picked up something white and fluttering alongside the road up ahead. At first he thought it was just a trick of his tired eyes, but as he drew closer he could make out the figure of a girl wearing a long, white dress. She was standing there in the rain trying to hitch a ride. Tired as he was, there was no way Jim could possibly ignore such a pathetic-looking creature.

He stopped the car just a few feet from the hitchhiker,

and as she walked up to the window he got a good look at her. She couldn't have been more than sixteen or seventeen years old. Her hair was drenched and hung limply over her face, and she looked miserable, though it was clear that she could be quite pretty under better conditions. Worst of all, her thin white, party dress was completely inadequate for the weather. She was shivering visibly.

"This is a bad place to try to get a ride, particularly at this time of night," said Jim.

"I know," she replied quietly. "I feel as if I have been standing here forever."

Jim asked the girl where she was going, and she gave him an address on the northwest side of Chicago. Jim told her she was lucky, because he had to go right by that area, and would be able to drop her off at her front door.

The girl asked Jim if he would mind if she got into the backseat of the car and lay down for a nap, as she was very tired. That was fine with him, so she climbed into the backseat of Jim's two-door Chevy. She thanked him again, and then apparently curled up on the backseat to sleep, for he heard nothing more from her.

Naturally, Jim was curious as to why the girl was standing out on a deserted road in the middle of a rainy night. But she didn't seem anxious to talk about her predicament, and he didn't want to pry. "I'll just do my good deed and go home," he thought.

It was about thirty miles from the spot where Jim had picked up the girl to the address in the city she had given him. He had no trouble finding the place.

He pulled up in front of a modest, brick house. "I guess this is it," he said. "You're probably glad to get home."

There was no response. "This is the place, isn't it?" he said more loudly. Still no response. Jim turned and looked at the backseat. It was empty!

Quickly, Jim went over the events in his mind. He had picked up the girl and she got into the backseat of a two-door car. He had driven nonstop for about thirty miles. There was no possible way that anyone could have gotten out of the car, yet she was gone.

For a moment Jim toyed with the idea of simply driving away, and trying to forget the whole thing. But this was a mystery he could not ignore. Slowly and reluctantly, he got out of the his car and went up to the front door of the brick house. He rang the bell and waited, a bit apprehensively. After a few seconds, a light inside was switched on, and he heard footsteps coming toward the door. When the door opened, a middle-aged couple, who had obviously just gotten out of bed, stared out at him. "Yes, what is it?" said the man.

For a moment, Jim didn't know what to say. "Look, I'm really sorry to wake you up at this time of night, but about the girl who lives here . . ." Jim was unable to finish, for the couple stared at him with a mixture of anger and horror.

"We live here alone," said the man. "No girl lives here."

"I must have made some sort of mistake," said Jim. He was about to turn and leave when he saw a framed photograph on the wall, behind the couple. The face was bright, smiling, and very pretty, but it was, without a doubt, the face of the hitchhiking girl in the white dress. "That girl, the girl in the photograph on the wall, that's who I'm talking about."

The woman screamed, and the man clenched his fists as if he were about to hit Jim.

"I don't know what you think you're doing, young man," he growled. "That's a picture of our daughter. She was killed in an automobile accident, about thirty miles north of here, exactly one year ago."

You may have heard that story, or something very like it, before. It's called "The Phantom Hitchhiker," and it is without a doubt the most famous and widely told ghost story in America, perhaps in the world. No one knows where or how this story began, or how much truth there may be behind it. All we do know is that a lot of people have believed in hitchhiking ghosts, and have for a long time.

There are a tremendous number of variations of the

phantom hitchhiker story, some quite old. Here are just a few.

This one goes back to the days when freight was hauled by teams of horses pulling large wagons. The men who drove such wagons were called teamsters. That name has carried over to the modern freight hauler, the truck driver.

There was a teamster who hauled freight along the back roads of upstate New York. He was known as "a tremendous fellow, afraid of neither man, beast, nor the Devil; night or day, it made no difference to him." On one particularly nasty, stormy night, he was hauling a load and had to stop for a moment. A man emerged from the darkness, and climbed up on the wagon beside him. The stranger never said a word; he just sat there.

The big teamster wasn't frightened, just puzzled. He looked over at the stranger to see whether he should kick him off the wagon, but he couldn't see much because it was very dark, and the man had his hat pulled down and his coat collar turned up. The teamster decided that this was no place for a fight, so the two of them drove on for about a mile, neither saying a word.

Then, quite suddenly, the stranger fell over sideways off the wagon, like a sack. The teamster went up to a nearby farmhouse, and he and the farmer searched the dark road with lanterns, looking for the man. But they couldn't find any trace of him.

The whole incident would have been forgotten, were it not for the fact that three months later, the big teamster was found lying dead at the side of the road. His neck had been broken. It was the exact spot where the stranger had fallen from the wagon.

Another story from about the same time concerns a laborer everyone called Red. Red had to walk about four miles from his home to the place where he was working. Often, while walking along the road, Red was overtaken by a man driving an old-fashioned buggy. Sometimes the two would exchange a few words, and then the buggy would drive off. One night, when it was raining very hard, the buggy driver offered to give Red a lift. It was an offer Red gratefully accepted.

This evening the buggy driver seemed to be unusually quiet. Red tried to start a conversation, but got no response. The driver had his face buried deep in his upturned coat collar. When he finally did turn and face Red, the sight was shocking. The driver's eyes were greenish and glowed with an unnatural light, and his skin was pale with the pallor of death.

"What's wrong?" exclaimed Red. "Are you sick?"

The driver said nothing. He just stared at Red, and as he did, his face began to change and gave off an unearthly glow. Then the driver disappeared. The horse became frightened and excited, and bolted. It was all Red could do to get the buggy under control. He was finally able to stop the runaway horse, and got out of the buggy. The moment his foot touched the ground, the driver reappeared and drove off.

Here is another tale that is about a hundred years old. A couple of farmers were driving down the road in their wagon when they spotted a boy sitting on a milestone at the crossroads.

The boy came up to the wagon and asked the farmers if they were heading for the village. They assured him that they were. He then asked them if they would take a message to his parents, as he would not be able to get home as quickly as expected. The farmers said that they would, so the boy gave them the message and the address. As they started down the road, one of the farmers looked back. The crossroad was wide open, there was no possible hiding place, yet the boy seemingly had disappeared. The farmers were puzzled, but didn't think much of it—until later.

In town they found the address that they had been given and knocked on the door. A woman answered.

"Does the Torcelli family live here?" one of the farmers asked.

"Yes, I am Mrs. Torcelli," the woman said.

"We have a message from your son."

At that, the woman's face turned ashen, and she rushed back into the house. A few seconds later her husband appeared, and began to yell at the farmers about cruel, practical jokes. The farmers were completely taken aback. They thought they were doing the family a favor by delivering a message.

They protested that they meant no harm, and when the man had calmed a bit, they gave him the message that the boy had given to them:

"The documents you have been searching for are in the top drawer of the bureau. You have already looked in the drawer, but you neglected to check under the paper at the bottom of the drawer."

Mr. Torcelli looked suspicious, but he went back into the house. A moment later there was a shout, and he returned waving some papers in his hand.

He was very apologetic, and tried to explain. Six months earlier, his son had been killed in an accident at the crossroads. In the despair and confusion caused by the death, Mr. Torcelli had misplaced the deed for some family property, and someone else claimed the property. The Torcelli family had practically torn the house apart, without success, until the farmers delivered the message.

Eleanor Tabori was driving home late one night. The road was deserted and the weather was beginning to turn nasty. She glanced down at her gas gauge, and the needle was quivering on Empty. She knew she was low on gas, but she didn't figure she was that low. There probably wouldn't be a gas station open at this time of night. But she consoled herself with the thought that it was only a few more miles before she was home, and there was always a little gas in the tank even when it registered Empty. She would probably have enough gas to make it—probably.

As she came over the top of a hill, her headlights picked up the figure of a man standing at the side of the road. He was wearing a long, gray overcoat, and had his thumb stuck out. He was hitchhiking. As she drew nearer, Eleanor got a closer look at the man. He had a vacant, almost crazed expression on his square, unshaven face. Eleanor, who thought it was dangerous to pick up hitchhikers anyway, certainly wasn't about to give a lift to anyone who looked like that, particularly in the middle of the night.

The man in the gray coat caught Eleanor's eye as she drove past. It was a chilling glance, and she was glad when he was out of sight. But as Eleanor came over the top of another hill, she saw another figure standing at the side of the road. And as she drew closer, she had a sickening realization. This was not another hitchhiker, it was exactly the same man she had seen just a mile or so back. There was no way he could possibly have gotten ahead of her, yet there he was, and he was staring directly at her. His lips were drawn back from his teeth in a hideous smile.

Eleanor pressed the accelerator to the floor and swept on past him in a surge of power. As she glanced down

at the gas gauge, the needle gave a slight shudder and came to rest just below Empty.

"Oh, please, it isn't far now. There must be some gas left, there must be!" she thought.

Eleanor's car climbed another hill, and it felt like it was slowing down, as if it were running out of gas, though that may have been Eleanor's frantic imagination.

As she came over the crest of the hill, she was afraid to look over to the side of the road, but she had to. There was the man in the gray coat once again. This time there had been a change. Before, he had been sticking his thumb out. His hand was still extended, but now he seemed to be holding something. As she got closer, Eleanor realized what it was he was holding. It was a large knife.

Now the car really was slowing down. Eleanor could feel it, and the engine was sputtering, as if starved for fuel. She was close to home; if the car could only make it over the next hill, she could actually coast right into her own driveway, and then she would be safe. Would the car make it?

The sheriff found Eleanor's body slumped over the wheel of her car. She had been stabbed to death. The sheriff figured she had picked up a hitchhiker who killed her. It was strange that there was no sign of robbery. Needless to say, the murderer was never apprehended.

*   *   *

Two salesmen were driving along a country road when they spotted a most unusual hitchhiker. She was a very respectable-looking, middle-aged lady. Though they didn't usually pick up hitchhikers, they stopped to pick up this one.

The hitchhiker chatted amiably about the weather and other inoffensive topics. She was so perfectly respectable-looking and -sounding that the salesmen didn't feel right about asking her why she was hitch-hiking.

They drove along for a couple of miles until the woman said, "I get out at the crossroads right up ahead."

As she departed, she thanked the salesmen for the ride, and quite unexpectedly said, "Within an hour you'll have a dead man in your car." She then walked off rapidly, leaving behind two stunned and speechless salesmen.

They continued their journey. About forty-five minutes later, they saw a lot of flashing red lights. The lights belonged to a couple of police cars and an ambulance. There had been a horrible multi-vehicle accident, with several serious injuries.

The police stopped the salesmen's car and explained that there had been so many injuries that they needed help in getting people to the hospital. Could they possibly take someone? The salesmen had no choice but to agree. The police helped one of the victims, who did not appear to be too badly injured, into the car. As it turned out, the man was far more badly hurt than he looked, and he died on his way to the hospital, as the salesmen knew he would.

2

Big Joe

Randy Talbot stood in the dark, staring vacantly down the empty highway. It was beginning to rain, and there wasn't much traffic on this road at night, so his chances of getting a ride seemed slim. It looked like another night spent in the open, cold and hungry. Randy was feeling about as low as he ever had in his life.

Randy had half-run away, half-been kicked out of his home at the age of fifteen. Try as he might, he couldn't remember a single really good day in those fifteen years. Life had been an unending string of arguments and fights, and when he wasn't fighting with his parents, a sullen silence reigned. They never talked, not even to say hello.

Randy sometimes wondered if his parents missed him, or even noticed he was gone. He certainly didn't miss them. But three years on his own had been no picnic. He had hitchhiked all over the country, sometimes sleeping in abandoned buildings or doorways. He picked up an odd job now and then; he also panhandled, shoplifted, and robbed to get enough to eat. He wasn't a violent kid; he was just trying to get by in a very tough world.

Randy kept on moving because he never found any place he really wanted to stay. He always hoped the next place would be better than the last. It never was; it was just more of the same. Now he felt his string about run out. He was standing in the rain, on a deserted road in Iowa. He hadn't eaten in over twenty-four hours, and he had no idea where he was going, or what he was going to do when he got there, if he got there. He didn't really care anymore.

It was the roar of the truck he heard first. There was a big eighteen-wheeler laboring up the incline. Then he saw the lights. Randy was almost too discouraged to stick out his thumb. The driver probably wouldn't stop anyway, he thought, but the truck ground to a halt right in front of him. The trucker leaned out of the window and said, "Where you going, kid?"

"No place special," replied Randy. "Just down the road, I guess."

"That's where I'm going, too. Get in."

Randy climbed into the cab and settled himself alongside the driver. He couldn't get a good look at the man, but he could tell that he was big, and he had a deep, commanding voice.

"Lousy place to try to catch a ride," said the big man. "How'd you wind up here?"

Years of being on his own had made Randy deeply suspicious of strangers. He didn't like talking to them. They always wanted something from you. But the big trucker with the deep voice inspired immediate confidence and trust. Usually Randy answered questions with a single word or a grunt; now he found the words pouring out of him. He began telling this complete stranger his whole life story. And though he still couldn't see the driver's face, he knew the big man was listening.

Randy had just about run out of words when he saw the bright lights of a truck stop up ahead. The driver pulled into the parking lot and stopped. "You've had it real rough," said the driver. "But don't give up hope. You're young, you've got time, and you never can tell what's going to happen. I've got to turn off up ahead. You get out here." The trucker shoved a five-dollar bill into Randy's hand. "Get yourself something to eat. The food's not bad in this place, and the apple pie is terrific. Tell 'em Big Joe dropped you off. They know me, and they'll treat you right."

Randy climbed down out of the cab. Before he even had a chance to thank his benefactor, the rig pulled out of the lot and disappeared down the road. Suddenly

Randy began to cry. This was the first act of real kindness he had ever experienced in his life, and he was overwhelmed with emotion.

After he got control of himself, Randy went into the diner, and ordered a cheeseburger and fries, which he polished off greedily. Then he said to the counterman, "I'll have some apple pie. Big Joe tells me you have real good apple pie."

"So Big Joe dropped you off here," said the counterman.

"Yeah, he's a real nice guy. You know him well?"

"You never heard of Big Joe?"

Randy admitted that he hadn't.

"Fifteen years ago, Big Joe was driving down this very road, when a school bus going in the opposite direction went out of control, and was coming right for him. Joe swerved off the road to avoid the bus. Nobody on the bus was hurt, but Joe got killed.

"Since then, every once in a while a down-and-out hitchhiker like yourself gets picked up by Joe. He gives them a couple of bucks and drops them off here for a meal. I guess you could say he was a real nice guy, and still is. Consider yourself lucky, kid. I think he's giving you a second chance."

3

The Caretaker Who Wouldn't Leave

It was to be a happy camping vacation for the Cartwright family of South Yorkshire in England. Jack Cartwright, his wife, June, and their two children, thirteen-year-old Melissa and eleven-year-old Alan, were to spend two weeks camping in the West Country. But everything that could go wrong did. The weather was awful, and the whole family caught colds. While they were out hiking, vandals ransacked their tent. To top things off, their car began acting up. Something was wrong with the electrical system. The Cartwrights decided enough was enough. They packed up their gear and started home.

The bad luck that had dogged them from the start continued. They had to stop several times to repair the car. The weather, which had been threatening all day, erupted with a violent thunderstorm. Jack could barely see the road because of the sheets of rain, and with his vision limited, he missed his turnoff, and found himself driving down a narrow country lane.

By now it was getting dark, and the headlights were beginning to dim as the car's electrical system seemed about to fail completely. Their only hope was to find some sort of shelter for the night, but the area was so deserted that shelter appeared a remote possibility.

As the family just about resigned themselves to spending the night crammed into a stalled car, Alan shouted that he could see some buildings just up ahead. It was an abandoned railway yard. The British countryside is littered with such abandoned yards, relics of an era when most people rode trains instead of using automobiles.

Jack took his flashlight and got out of the car to examine the station. It was a big old building, now completely boarded-up. It had been well-built, and even after years of neglect, the roof was sound. He figured that if they could pry open one of the windows, the family could take their sleeping bags and be reasonably dry and comfortable inside.

The Cartwrights moved what they needed into what was once the ticket office. They were able to prepare a halfway decent meal, the rain stopped, and everybody began to feel better. Jack suggested that they explore their surroundings, for they had been cooped up in the car all day, and a little exercise would be good and help them sleep.

With their flashlights, the Cartwrights examined the broken, rubbish-strewn platform, and the tracks, now overgrown with weeds. The sense of desolation was complete and oppressive. And there was something else, a vague feeling of not quite being alone.

The children, who had gone ahead, came back shouting that they saw a light and heard voices. Their father assured them this was impossible, but the children were insistent and they led their parents to a small building, which had probably once been the freight office. Jack looked in through the window. The room inside was empty except for a few broken and dust-covered pieces of furniture and other discarded items.

"This is the place, Dad," Melissa insisted. "There was a yellowish light like an old oil lamp, and we heard voices."

The door to the building was either locked or had rusted shut. It could not be budged. Jack pried open the window and climbed in. There was nothing but the undisturbed dust of years of disuse. Yet there was a strange, undefinable smell, quite apart from the smell of dust and mildew. And there was the strong feeling of not being alone. Jack felt genuinely frightened and got out of the building as quickly as he could. He didn't tell his family of his fears. He simply assured them that the building was quite empty, and the light and voices must have been an illusion.

Within half an hour, the Cartwright family was in their sleeping bags, trying to sleep, but they all felt uneasy, though no one could say exactly why. Finally, Jack drifted off into a troubled sleep. At about 2:00 A.M., he awoke with a start. This was no dream or illusion; he did hear voices coming from the baggage office. He pulled on a pair of pants, grabbed his flashlight, and went to investigate.

As Jack approached the old baggage office, the sound of voices became louder, and he could see a yellowish glow filtering through the grimy windows. He tried the door. It was as firmly locked as before, but when he put his shoulder to it, the door fairly sprang open, and Jack found himself in the middle of a misty glow, looking at a figure sitting in a chair at a desk. The whole scene was very indistinct, but the figure appeared to be poring over a pile of papers. Though it was hard to make out the details, the rubbish that had once filled the room had been replaced by furniture of an earlier era. It was like stepping back into the past. For a moment, Jack was stunned, unable to move.

The figure at the desk turned and looked at him. This was no skull-faced ghostly horror, but the deeply wrinkled face of a gentle-looking old man wearing old-fashioned, steel-rimmed glasses. He smiled at Jack, who took a step forward. Then, abruptly, the whole scene

vanished. Jack had returned to the dark, dusty, rubbish-filled office of the present. And the door behind him was locked once again. There was a moment of panic, until Jack remembered the window he had opened earlier. It was still open. He climbed through, went back to the main station, crawled into his sleeping bag, and tried, without much success, to go back to sleep. It was with great relief that he greeted the first faint light of dawn.

In the morning, he recounted his experience to his wife, June, who obviously didn't believe a word of what he was saying and tried to reassure him that it had all been nothing more than a bad dream brought on by the strains of the day and the unfamiliar and spooky surroundings. And by the light of day, the whole experience did take on a dreamlike quality. Jack went back to the freight office and looked inside. It was a long-deserted room, with absolutely nothing unusual about it.

The Cartwrights left the old station in search of a garage where they hoped to be able to get their car repaired. They found a nearby garage, and while waiting for the work to be done, Jack told the owner that the family had spent the night at the deserted station. He said nothing about the vision of the old man, or the other strange events.

"You're a braver man than I am," said the garage owner. "That station is supposed to be haunted by old

Garrity, who worked at the place for as long as anyone could remember. The day the station was scheduled to close down for good, they found the old man sitting in his office, dead. Some people say he has never left. Folks around here won't go near the place in the daytime, let alone at night."

"I don't know what they're afraid of," laughed Jack. But his laugh was forced. As soon as the car was repaired, Jack Cartwright and his family left the area as quickly as they could. And they never came back.

4

Roadside Phantoms

It is said that the spirits of people who died a violent death often haunt the spot at which the death occurred. There are many drivers who will swear that they met the restless ghost of an accident victim or some other unfortunate person who died violently, at the spot on the road where they died.

A British truck driver named Harold Unsworth was traveling along his regular route one evening a few years ago when he stopped to pick up a young man who was hitchhiking. The hitchhiker asked for a lift to a place called the Old Beam Bridge, just a few miles down the road. Unsworth was happy to help out.

The young man didn't turn out to be the best of companions. All during the ride, he recounted, in the most gory imaginable detail, stories of the accidents that were supposed to have happened at the bridge. Unsworth was happy to see his morbid companion leave, once they reached the bridge.

A few months later, Unsworth was traveling the same route when he spotted the same hitchhiker, at the same spot. Since the young man had not been very pleasant the first time, the truck driver was tempted to pass him by. But Harold Unsworth was basically a kind-hearted fellow, and he knew that the road was pretty deserted and that the hitchhiker might not get a ride for hours. So he stopped his truck, and the young man climbed in again, and again said that he wanted to go to the Old Beam Bridge.

As before, the hitchhiker's conversation was a bloody account of horrible accidents at the bridge. This time, when the truck got to the bridge, the hitchhiker said he wanted to go a little farther down the road, but he had to pick up a few things he had left at the bridge. Would Unsworth please wait a moment for him? Now it was late, and Unsworth was tired and anxious to finish work and go home. But he was too polite to say anything but, "Sure, I'll wait a moment for you."

Unsworth waited and waited, but the hitchhiker didn't come back. Finally, his patience ran out and he swore if he ever saw that particular hitchhiker again he would pass him by.

He got his chance about three miles later, for there by the side of the road stood the very same hitchhiker, with his thumb out. Unsworth couldn't figure out how the guy got up the road that fast. But he knew that he wasn't going to pick him up. So rather than slowing down, he speeded up, just to let the fellow know that he wasn't going to get any more rides in that truck.

Suddenly, the hitchhiker jumped out into the road right in front of the truck. Unsworth slammed on the brakes, but there was no way he could stop in time. He was sure he hit the hitchhiker, though he didn't feel any impact. Then Unsworth looked in his rearview mirror. He saw the hitchhiker, apparently uninjured, standing in the middle of the road, shaking a fist at him. The truck driver did not stick around to investigate.

Unsworth never was able to come up with a reasonable, or even unreasonable, explanation for what had happened. His best guess was that the hitchhiker was a ghost. Perhaps the ghost of one of the victims of the accidents at the Old Beam Bridge that he had described so colorfully.

Paul Corey was driving to his home in a suburb just outside of Cleveland. It was late and he was very tired. Perhaps he wasn't being as attentive to his surroundings as usual. In any case, as he came over the crest of the hill, he suddenly saw the figure of a young girl directly in his headlights. She seemed to be standing right in the middle of the road. She made no attempt to move; the headlights may have blinded her. Paul

slammed on the brakes, but there was no chance of stopping in time. He hit the girl, though the impact was not as hard as he had feared.

Paul immediately stopped his car and rushed over to the girl, who was lying at the side of the road. It was clear that she was badly hurt. There was a lot of blood around her head and face. She was unconscious but breathing.

For a moment, Paul didn't know what to do. He remembered, or tried to remember, all those things he had been taught in first aid class. One of the things he remembered clearly was that you aren't supposed to move a person who has been seriously injured. He recalled being told that the best thing to do was cover the injured person, and call for professional help.

Paul had a blanket in his car, with which he covered the girl. He didn't have a phone in his car, and he didn't know how long he would have to wait for someone else to come along to get help. He figured that there wasn't much traffic on this particular road late at night. He might have to wait for an hour or more, and by that time the injured girl would bleed to death.

He decided that the best course of action was to leave the girl, and drive to the state police headquarters, which he knew was only a few miles away.

The police rushed to the scene of the accident. When they got there, they found only a blanket on the ground. However, there was some blood on the blanket. Paul was questioned at length by suspicious policemen. He simply repeated his story. The next morning the police searched the area with the aid of bloodhounds. They couldn't find any trace of an injured girl. Nor were there any reports of a missing girl.

The police would have dismissed Paul's experience as an hallucination, but in checking their records they found that a young girl had been struck and killed by a hit-and-run driver at that same spot some fifteen years earlier. At least two other drivers had reported experiences similar to Paul's.

During the late 1930s, there were tales of a phantom bus in London. It would appear in the most alarming possible way. A driver would be coming along St. Mark's Road, just minding his own business, when suddenly he would see this gigantic double-decker bus careening toward him. By the time he saw the bus there was absolutely nothing that could be done. All the hapless driver could do was hit on the brakes, wait for the crash, and pray, if he was a praying man.

It's possible that some nonbelievers became instant converts to the power of prayer, for there was no crash. The bus simply disappeared. The phantom bus caused a couple of accidents, when drivers swerved in an attempt to get out of the way.

Luckily, there were no serious accidents until June 11, 1933. Because of the sighting of the phantom bus, one of the drivers crashed head-on into another car. The driver of the second car was killed. After that, there were no more sightings of the ghost bus. Perhaps its obscure, but deadly, mission had finally been fulfilled after it claimed a victim.

Lord Halifax was a great collector of ghostly accounts in the early years of this century. This one he attributed to a Captain Wintour, who lived in the county of York-shire.

The captain had been out hunting one day, and he was driving his small carriage to the house of a friend.

"I had a drive of some fourteen miles to make and at one point had to cross a bridge over a stream. As I approached, I saw a man leaning over the railing and looking down into the river below. Noticing that he had a bag at his side, and thinking he might be tired, I stopped the cart I was driving and offered to give him a lift if he was going in my direction. He climbed into the cart without a word and sat there in silence. I made two attempts to draw him into conversation, but gave up trying when he made no sign of responding."

They drove along in silence for some time, until they came to a village. By that time it was quite dark. The inn in the village was well lighted, and some people were standing in front. One of the people who worked in the inn came forward to take Captain Wintour's horse.

"My companion got down and without one word of thanks to me walked straight into the inn. 'Who was that man who has just climbed down?' I asked the fellow who was holding my horse. He replied that he had not seen anyone. 'Well, the man I drove up with,' I said; to which he replied, 'You drove up alone, Sir.' "

This made Captain Wintour feel very uncomfortable, as you can imagine. He found the owner of the inn. "When I told him of my companion and described him, he looked grave and asked me to follow him upstairs. He took me into a room and there on the bed lay the man to whom I had given a lift. He was dead, and had been dead for some time; in fact, an inquest had just been held on his body. A day or two earlier he had been found drowned in the stream, close to the bridge where I had first seen him."

Traditionally, the ghost seen at the place where a violent death took place is that of the person who died there. But in one singular case from England, the ghost seems to have been that of a grieving family member.

On a quiet road between Marlborough and Hungerford is a small stone cross inscribed with these words: "A.P. Watts, May 12, 1879." It was a memorial to a fourteen-year-old boy, Alfie Watts, who had died tragically at that spot. The boy had been working for a man who hauled heavy loads with a large horse-drawn cart. One day the horses bolted, and the boy tried to stop them, but he fell beneath the wheels of the cart and died a few hours later. Villagers erected the small stone monument to his memory.

Over the years memories fade, and the cross itself was often nearly hidden by grass and wild flowers. Then, in October of 1956, Frederick Moss and three friends were driving home from the movies when their headlights picked up a tall, thin, clean-shaven man standing in the middle of the road. He wore a long, brown coat and stood with his back to the spot where the cross was almost hidden in the grass.

Moss blew his horn. The man in the road didn't even react, much less get out of the way. The driver angrily slammed on his brakes and got out to curse the man in the road as a dangerous fool. But no one was there. Moss suddenly had the awful feeling that he might have hit the fellow. With his companions, he searched the area, but found nothing. There were steep walls on either side of the road and it seemed impossible that anyone could have climbed up one of them without being seen.

Moss was deeply shaken by what had happened and later told the story to his wife. She had been born in the area, though it was many years after the accident which had killed little Alfie Watts. Still, she remembered his father, Henry Pounds Watts, who died in 1907. The figure her husband described sounded like the Henry Watts that she remembered.

Why had he suddenly chosen to appear after all those years? There was a plan to widen the road, and if that was done, the little cross might be destroyed. The father may have wanted to remind people that the modest memorial to his son should be preserved when the road construction took place.

If that was the ghost's mission, it certainly succeeded, for when the road was widened, the little cross was carefully replaced nearby.

5

Strangers on a Train

On a Friday night in July of 1935, Stanley Paris was going to visit some friends in the country. Paris was a busy man, and he had put some important business papers in his briefcase, intending to read them during the trip. When he arrived at Euston Station in London, he asked the guard for an empty compartment where he could read without being disturbed. In some British trains, and many trains on the European continent as well, cars are divided into individual compartments, each with its own door which can be locked.

The guard found Paris an empty compartment and apparently locked the door to insure his privacy. But just before the train pulled out, a very respectable-looking elderly man, carrying a small black leather bag, boarded and entered the compartment. Paris was a bit annoyed at first, but the latecomer sat quietly and did not disturb him. After a short time, Paris found that he was unable to concentrate on his reading, and he fell into conversation with the man sharing his compartment.

It turned out that the old gentleman was one of the directors of the railway company. Paris speculated that this was why he was able to get into a supposedly locked compartment. The fellow proved to be remarkably chatty. He told Paris that he was very interested in a new branch line that was about to be opened. He also said that he was carrying £70,000, a huge sum of the railway company's money. He was to deposit the money in a bank to pay for work that had just been completed. As he talked about the money, he patted the black leather bag, as if to indicate that was where the money was being carried.

"Aren't you afraid," said Paris, "to carry such a large sum of money with you?"

"Oh, no," came the reply. "No one would know. Besides, who would rob me? Certainly not you, just because I have told you. I am not afraid of anything."

Paris was less talkative about his own business affairs, but he did tell his fellow traveler that he was going down to the country and where he would be staying.

"By the way," the old gentleman said, "I know that house you are visiting. The lady of the house is my niece. Tell her that I hope the next time I come to stay she won't have such a huge fire in the Blue Room. She nearly roasted me last time."

As the train drew into the next station, the old gentleman announced that this was where he got off. He took a business card out of his pocket and gave it to Paris. The name Dwerringhouse was printed on the card. After his fellow traveler left the train, Paris noticed an expensive cigar case on the floor of the compartment. He assumed that Dwerringhouse had dropped it. Sure enough, he could see Dwerringhouse's name engraved on the case. He picked it up and ran out to the platform, hoping to return the case to its owner.

Paris caught a brief glimpse of Dwerringhouse at the far end of the platform talking to a man. Paris was able to get a pretty good look at the second man, and noted that he had very distinctive sandy-colored hair. Then unaccountably, Paris lost sight of the two men. It was almost as if they had disappeared into thin air. The porter on the platform was no help, and said that he had not seen either of the men.

Stanley Paris pocketed the cigar case and returned to his compartment. He was puzzled by what had happened, but there seemed nothing he could do about it.

When he got to his destination, Paris remembered the message that he was supposed to give to his hostess.

"I traveled down on the train with an uncle of yours," he said. "He asked me to tell you that the next time he comes to stay, you shouldn't have such a huge fire in the Blue Room."

This simple, and rather inoffensive, message seemed to upset the woman so much that she had to leave the room. Her husband took Paris aside and explained that this was all very embarrassing. The uncle, Mr. Dwerringhouse, had disappeared some months earlier. What was worse, he had taken £70,000 of the railway company's money with him. Though the whole incident had been kept very quiet, the police were looking for Dwerringhouse, but had been unable to find any trace of him.

"As you can imagine, it is not a pleasant subject in this house," said the husband.

It so happened that among the guests at the country house that weekend were two directors of the railway company. They overheard the conversation, and afterwards asked Paris if he could give them any more information about the man he had met on the train.

"No," replied Paris, "I can't tell you anything else, except that I saw him and talked with him and left him, as I thought, speaking to another man on the platform of the station where we parted."

The directors continued to press him, and eventually they asked if he would mind appearing before a full meeting of the board of directors and tell his story to them. Somewhat reluctantly, Paris agreed.

In due course, the meeting was arranged. Paris felt a little foolish standing in front of a distinguished-looking group in a very elegant room, telling this rather simple and, he thought, pointless story. In the middle of his narrative he suddenly stopped and exclaimed, "There is the man I saw talking to Mr. Dwerringhouse—that man with the sandy hair!"

A sandy-haired man actually was sitting among the directors. He was the cashier of the railway company. He was completely taken by surprise when Paris pointed him out.

"But I wasn't there," he called out. "I was away on my vacation."

The other directors insisted that the company records be examined. It was soon clear that the cashier had not been away on vacation as he had stated. The police were called in and, within a few hours, the cashier broke down and confessed everything.

The cashier said that he had been embezzling money from the railway company for years, but he was afraid that he would not be able to cover up his crime much longer. He knew that Dwerringhouse was going to be carrying a large sum of company money in cash. The cashier said he had intended to steal the money and leave the country. He met the old man at the station, and persuaded him to take a short cut through a quarry, and knocked him on the head. He had only meant to stun the old man, and so get possession of his bag. When he fell, Dwerringhouse struck his head on a rock and was killed.

With this turn of events, the cashier changed his plans. He hid the body, and used the cash to replace

what he had embezzled. The plan seemed to work perfectly for months; all suspicion had centered on the missing Dwerringhouse. Then, unaccountably, the scene of the meeting of the murderer and his victim had been reenacted on a railway platform before the eyes of Stanley Paris.

And what about the cigar case? It is very rare in ghostly encounters that the ghost leaves behind any physical evidence. When the police examined all the circumstances surrounding the case, they discovered that the carriage in which Paris had traveled had been taken out of service, for routine repairs, on the day on which Dwerringhouse had disappeared. It had been put back into service for the first time on the day that Paris made his journey. It seemed probable that the murdered man was the last passenger to ride in the compartment before it was taken out of service. He may well have dropped his cigar case at that time, and Paris was the first to see it.

The guard at Euston Station in London was also closely questioned. He was positive that on the day of the appearance he had locked the door of the compartment, and that when the train started, Stanley Paris had been alone in the compartment.

6

What Was It?

Imagine this: You are driving along a deserted and lonely road one night. Suddenly, your headlights pick up something along the side of the road. At first, you can't make out what it is. But as you draw closer, you are able to get a better look at it. To your horror, you realize that the thing at the side of the road is like nothing you have ever seen before. Whatever it is, it is something that shouldn't be on this road, or any road ever. Without warning, the thing rushes out into the road in front of you, and you get a good look at it in the full glare of your headlights. You wish you hadn't.

People from all over the world have been reporting experiences like this for many years. What are they seeing, or think they are seeing? Lots of different things.

Take the experience reported by twenty-one-year-old Margaret Johnson. On a spring night in 1966, she and her boyfriend were driving down a lonely road near the town of Drogheda in Ireland.

"Suddenly, John was forced to brake hard as a horse loomed up before us. I was thrown back on the seat. When I looked out the window, I saw this monster or ghost or whatever it was. I could see by John's face that he saw it too. I think I screamed, but both of us were so frightened that we were paralyzed. The thing had a horse's body. But it was the face, leering and hairy and huge, which shocked. The animal stretched right across the road and completely blocked the car. It stayed for nearly two minutes. We were petrified. Then it vanished. John quickly swung the car around and drove to my home, about a mile away. We were so frightened that we drove through the gate and knocked it off the hinges."

Or take the experience reported in a 1967 letter to the editor of the *Winona* (Mississippi) *Times*. It came from a Georgia man who signed himself only as J.H.

According to J.H., he and his brother were driving their pickup truck to Marietta, Georgia, on November 7, 1966. At about one-thirty in the morning, they were on the highway between the towns of Eupora and Winona, Mississippi. The headlights of the pickup illuminated a figure running along the side of the road. It was about seven feet tall and covered with hair. J.H.'s first thought was that the thing was a bear. But bears don't run on two legs—not for very long anyway. The creature was holding up one arm, "like waving good-bye or giving a stop signal." The face of the creature, he said, "was like a person gone wild or crazy." It looked both human and animal.

J.H. and his brother agreed that the thing, whatever it was, appeared to be scared. Perhaps it was even signaling for help. But the men in the truck were also scared. They drove off as fast as they could, without bothering to investigate further.

J.H. went on to say that he had once been a prospector in the mountains of northern California. There he had heard many stories of the legendary monster called Bigfoot. He had always laughed at such stories. But since the thing he saw on the road looked a lot like the descriptions of Bigfoot, he wasn't laughing anymore.

In fact, many people, particularly in America, claim that they have seen a Bigfoot-like creature along the side of a deserted road. Sometimes the creature seems very solid and real.

On April 28, 1975, at three in the morning, Peter Hureuk was driving to his home in Pennsylvania. Suddenly, a hairy giant loomed up in front of his car. Hureuk couldn't avoid the thing. He struck it with his left front fender. It screamed and ran away, clutching at its side. There was a dent in the fender of his car, with what appeared to be a bit of fur sticking to it. Police

searched the area where the encounter was supposed to have taken place, but they could find nothing.

Others have reported actually hitting the creature head-on. But instead of the car-crunching impact they had expected, they passed right through it, as if it were some sort of ghost or phantom. A few brave souls said that they actually got out of their cars after such an encounter, fully expecting to find a dead, or mortally wounded, monster knocked off to the side of the road. Instead, they found nothing.

Similar tales have been told about encounters with a variety of other fantastical creatures along the roadside. In Britain, drivers have reported seeing a variety of phantom dogs for many years. Usually these dogs are huge, and black, with glowing red eyes. More than anything, they resemble the Hound of the Baskervilles, of the famous Sherlock Holmes tale. The dog will either be standing along the side of the road, staring at the driver. Or it will, suddenly and apparently suicidally, leap in front of the car. Of course, there is no impact, and no dog is ever found. In Britain it is considered very bad luck to see one of these phantom black dogs. According to some legends, people who see one are fated to die within a year.

Mountain lions, or pumas, have occasionally been reported prowling the roadsides of the American Midwest, where there very definitely should be no mountain lions. One thoroughly startled driver said one of the creatures actually jumped on the hood of his car. Whenever the police are called, no trace of a mountain lion can be found.

The same sort of stories have also been told about kangaroos. Now you may not think a kangaroo is a very frightening animal. And in truth, it isn't. But if you happen to be driving along a road in Indiana one night, and suddenly a giant kangaroo hops right out into the middle of the road, you are certainly going to be surprised. Greg Brothers was, when that happened to him in 1974.

One of the most extraordinary series of "What was it?" roadside encounters began on the night of November 14, 1966. Two young couples from Point Pleasant, West Virginia, were driving through an abandoned ammunition dump, known locally as the TNT area. It was located approximately seven miles outside of the town of Point Pleasant.

As they passed the empty powder plant, they saw something "shaped like a man but bigger" standing alongside the road. The thing seemed to have large wings folded against its back, and bright, almost luminous, red eyes. The driver of the car slowed down, and the four stared at it for about a minute, but it didn't appear to have any interest in them. The thing then turned away from the road, and walked, with a strange shuffling gait, back toward the door of the powder plant. This strange sight filled the occupants of the car with a sense of uneasiness, almost dread, and they didn't feel like hanging around to see what would happen. The driver stepped on the gas and sped away down Route 62.

Imagine their surprise, and terror, when they looked up in the sky and found that the winged thing was following them. It was flying overhead, and seemed to be pacing the car, though the driver swears that he was doing 100 mph after he spotted it. The thing made a squeaking noise "like a mouse." At the city limits, the flying creature veered off and disappeared.

That was the first encounter with a creature that was finally dubbed "Mothman." The creature didn't really look like a moth, but a popular TV series based on the Batman comics was running on television at the time, and the name stuck. Somehow or other, Mothman became identified with UFOs. There is a persistent human desire to link one mystery with another. But there was no real UFO connection. Mothman fits much more comfortably into the catalogue of roadside horrors, for most of the Mothman encounters took place while the victim was driving along some deserted West Virginia road.

The creature was almost always described as being between six and seven feet tall, and gray in color. It was standing at the side of the road. At the approach of the car, it might unfold its wings and rise straight up into the air "like a helicopter," according to one witness. Sometimes it flew away, but on other occasions, like the one described by eighteen-year-old Connie Carpenter, it made straight for the car. It flew directly at the windshield. She thought there was going to be a collision, but Mothman veered off at the last second.

"Those eyes!" she said. "They were very red, and once they were fixed on me, I couldn't take my own eyes off them. It's a wonder I didn't have a wreck."

Most people could only remember the eyes. Connie Carpenter got a closer look at the creature's face, though her description isn't too helpful. "It was horrible . . . like something out of a science-fiction movie."

The Mothman excitement in the Point Pleasant area lasted for a little over a year. Finally, people just stopped seeing it anymore. Or at least they stopped reporting it. Mothman joined that long list of unknown things that we sometimes see, or think we see, while driving along deserted roads at night.

So next time you're on one of those deserted roads at night, keep your eyes open and you may see somthing very strange. But it might be wise not to look too closely. It may be something that you really don't want to see.

7

The Annan Road
Horrors

A lot of people in different parts of the world have reported strange and terrifying experiences while driving along deserted roads at night. But none of the accounts on record is quite as terrifying, bizarre, and complete as the story told by two brothers, Dereck and Norman Ferguson, who were aged twenty-two and fourteen at the time of their encounter with the unknown.

The brothers had been taking a brief driving vacation in their native Scotland in April, 1962. They were returning late one evening to their home in the town of Annan, and had stopped for gas in the small town of Dumfries, shortly before midnight. Annan lay about fifteen miles down the road.

As the boys headed down the moonlit road, it appeared to be quite deserted, not at all unusual at that hour of the night. They had gone about a mile out of Dumfries when quite suddenly something—it looked like a large white bird—flew directly at the windshield. Dereck, who was doing the driving, swerved to avoid hitting the thing, but there was no impact. Whatever it was seemed to just disappear before it reached the car. And that was just the beginning.

The next appearance was far more alarming. It looked like an old woman rushing madly down the middle of the road. She seemed to be screaming and waving her arms wildly. Once again, a collision seemed inevitable, but this figure, too, disappeared just before hitting the car.

After that, things really got bad. There was a stream of wildly unearthly figures on the road: Gigantic cats, huge black dogs with glowing eyes, vulture-like birds, and some human or roughly human shapes. All of these apparitions loomed up at the side of the road and seemed to hurtle themselves at the car, and all disappeared just before the moment of impact. Even though it was now obvious that the forms were not solid, they looked solid enough, and Dereck zigzagged and swerved, trying to avoid them.

The Ferguson boys were assailed by more than just apparitions. The interior of the car suddenly became very cold, though the brothers were drenched with sweat from their ordeal.

The most terrifying manifestation was the feeling that something was trying to force the car off the road and into an accident.

When recalling the ordeal, Dereck reported, "My hands seemed to become very heavy, and it was as if some force were trying to gain control of the steering wheel; control of the car became increasingly difficult. We seemed to be suffocating and I opened the window to get some fresh air, but it was bitterly cold outside and I just hung onto the wheel as screaming, high-pitched laughter and cackling noises seemed to mark our predicament. I was absolutely certain that an attempt was being made to force us off the road, and I was equally certain that a fatal accident would result."

Finally, Dereck was forced to give in and stop the car, and immediately the brothers were hit by a powerful force that rocked the vehicle violently from side to side. The terrified brothers opened the car doors and jumped out. It was as if they had entered another, and far more peaceful world. Outside of the car all seemed tranquil. But they knew they couldn't stand by the side of the road forever, so they got back in the car. Once inside, the violent shaking and rocking began all over again. Once again there was the sound of horrible, ghostly laughter, and noises that sounded like dozens of fists were pounding on the outside of the car.

Dereck decided that the only thing that he could do was to continue to drive on to Annan, slowly and carefully, no matter what seemed to be going on around them. And so the car inched painfully down a highway that appeared to be filled with terrifying supernatural figures that loomed up suddenly on all sides, and threw themselves in front of the vehicle.

Finally, the Fergusons noticed a pair of glowing red lights up ahead, and on closer inspection, they saw that they were the taillights of a large truck. That was an enormous relief, for the truck was the first normal-looking object they had seen for some time. It was an indication that other human beings were also on the road to Annan. But relief quickly turned to fear when Dereck realized that he was approaching the truck much too quickly and had completely lost control of the car. He was unable to stop, slow, or swerve out of the way. A crash seemed unavoidable. But as had happened before, the truck vanished just before the crash. It was not a real truck, but another of the phantoms on the road that night.

That was the last of the apparitions. The Ferguson brothers reached Annan exhausted, but safe. The entire experience had taken about half an hour, though at the time both felt that they had been trapped on the road for hours.

Dereck remained convinced that if he had driven off the road or had stopped for any length of time, he and his brother probably would not have survived the experience. He wasn't sure what would have happened to them; it was just a feeling that it would have been horrible.

Later, Dereck Ferguson was told that hundreds of years ago, witchcraft had been commonly practiced in the area through which they had driven. Others said that a phantom truck like the one that he and his brother had encountered had occasionally been reported by others. But no one else had ever been subjected to the full range of Annan road horrors. Why had they been singled out? Dereck hadn't a clue, but in the future he avoided that road, particularly at night.

There is another road in the British Isles haunted by a strange phenomenon. It is known locally as "the hairy hands." On a particular stretch of road across the Devon moors, drivers have reported that something seems to grab hold of the wheel of their car and try to turn it off the road. A number of minor accidents have resulted. Some who have had this experience describe it simply as a force that tries to turn the wheel. Others insist that they have seen a pair of ghostly hairy hands—just hands—trying to grab the wheel.. That's where the name "hairy hands" came from, and it has stuck.

Stories like that have been around for a long time. Long before the age of the automobile, drivers of carriages and carts said that the hairy hands tried to turn their horses into a ditch, while they were on that particular stretch of road.

There is at least one death attributed to the hairy hands. A lone motorcyclist was coming down the road, and several people who watched him said that he was riding along normally. Then, suddenly, he began to act strangely. He looked as if he were fighting something invisible for the control of his motorcycle. The result was that the motorcycle went out of control and ran at full speed into a tree. The rider was killed instantly. A victim of the hairy hands, said the locals.

After the accident, the hairy hands became quite well known throughout Britain. A small army of engineers and other experts examined the stretch of road to try and determine if there was anything in the construction that would cause vehicles to go out of control. They could find nothing—nothing normal, that is—and the mystery remains.

8

The Warning Light

Back in the days of steam trains, there was a type of railroad workman known as a "bummer" brakeman. The "bummer" used to quite literally "bum around"— that is, he would go from one rail line to another as the spirit moved him. Most bummers were young men who were still restless and looking for adventure. They had not felt the need to settle down to a steady job. They had no family responsibilities and enjoyed the freedom of being able to see as much of the country as they liked. Since most rail lines were always in need of a good brakeman, bummers rarely had any trouble finding work.

One such bummer, Chuck Tolley by name, had a very scary experience that caused him to change the way he lived. Tolley was well known in upstate New

York. At one time or another, he had worked on practically every rail line in the area, and he showed no signs of settling down.

On a particularly nasty and rainy evening, Tolley was traveling to a new job. He was sitting in the caboose of a train. The caboose was the last car, the place where members of the crew would stay when they were off duty. Tolley was waiting for a friend of his, the regular brakeman on the run, to finish inspecting the cars. He expected his friend to come in at any moment, and the two would drink some coffee and swap stories about life on the railroad.

Tolley was just thinking about what a terrible night it was to be climbing around on the tops of cars, when the train hit a sharp curve. The rain had washed out part of the railbed and weakened the tracks, so that when the train rounded the curve, the first dozen cars were derailed. Since this was a freight train, there were no passengers to be injured. All the members of the crew were also uninjured, all except one. When the derailment occurred, Tolley's friend, the brakeman, had been on top of the train. He was thrown down between the cars. Tolley found him, or rather what was left of him on the ground near the track. His head had been cut off in the impact. Tolley and the members of the crew picked up the body, and put it in the baggage car. They couldn't find the head anywhere. Tolley went back up the line to warn off any train that might be following them. As soon as the track was repaired, the train went on.

The accident was a gruesome and terrible one, but not completely unexpected. Keeping the railroads running under all kinds of weather conditions could be a dangerous job, and many men lost their lives in similar accidents. Tolley knew and accepted the dangers. Yet seeing his friend killed in such a horrible way had its effect. The bummer brakeman began to think about settling down, perhaps getting married and having a family. Being young, he thought he had all the time in the world. Now he realized that the future was always uncertain.

Tolley became a fireman, and then an engineer. On an engineer's pay, he figured that he would be able to support a family. He still had to move around from place to place, but now he went where the company sent him, not where he felt like going. Still, he always tried to avoid the run where the accident happened. He wasn't a superstitious man, but he just didn't feel comfortable going back to a place which held such bad memories.

A few years after he had become an engineer, Tolley was assigned to that run. He objected, of course, but his boss just wouldn't listen. In the end, Tolley figured he had to take what he was given whether he liked it or not. By then, the trains were running a lot faster than when he had been a bummer brakeman. Still, every time he came to that curve where his friend had lost his head, Tolley slowed the train down in spite of himself, especially on rainy nights. "I'm not afraid," he would say. "I'm just being careful."

Tolley traveled on that run for several years, and nothing unusual ever happened. He was almost able to pass by the scene of the accident without thinking about it; almost, but not quite. One rainy March evening, as Tolley's train approached the fatal curve, he saw a red warning light on the track ahead. He brought the train to a grinding, screeching halt. He told his fireman to go up the line to investigate.

The fireman came back and said that he didn't see a red light or anything else unusual, and that they should just start the train up and go on. Tolley was not satisfied. He decided that he would investigate himself, though it was really not proper for an engineer to leave his train. As he climbed out of the cab, he saw a red light bobbing over the track. The light seemed to be comimg from an old-style red globe lantern, a type that trainmen had not used for years. Tolley's own white lantern was swinging by his side as he walked.

Tolley kept his eyes on the red light. As he drew closer, he could see the lower part of a man's body faintly illuminated in the glow. The body appeared to be wearing the regulation blue overalls of a brakeman.

Tolley ran forward and shouted, "What's the matter? What's wrong?"

There was no reply. Tolley raised his own lantern to

see why the other fellow didn't answer. The reason was obvious enough. The figure in the blue overalls carrying the old-style red globe lantern, had no head!

Then the figure disappeared. Tolley found himself standing there alone on the track, in the midst of a howling rainstorm. He knew the figure he had seen was that of his old brakeman friend. He also knew that the specter had appeared for some reason. Tolley walked up the track a little farther. Around a sharp bend, he found a large boulder that had been loosened by the March rains and had rolled onto the track. A collision with the boulder would have caused a terrible accident. Tolley knew that the headlights of his locomotive would never have picked up the boulder in time for him to stop. If it had not been for the red warning light, there surely would have been an accident.

The boulder was much too large for the train crew to remove from the track, and a special wrecking crew had to be called in. They got a big laugh out of Tolley's story of a headless brakeman. They simply thought that his nerves had been shattered by such a close call, and that he had been seeing things. Tolley, however, knew what he had seen. He also knew that he could never again work on the railroad. He had been given one warning; he might not get another.

That next morning Chuck Tolley handed in his resignation.

9

The Ghost of the Great North Road

Two hundred years ago the fastest traffic on Britain's Great North Road, which ran from Edinburgh to London, were the mail coaches. And the fastest coachman was Tom Driffield. When Driffield fell in love with young Nancy, the daughter of a Yorkshire farmer and whom everyone called Nance, her parents were delighted, despite the fact that he was some fifteen years older than their daughter. Driffield was not only at the top of his profession, he was also known as a man of exceptional kindness and generosity.

Nance herself was at first flattered by the coachman's attentions. To drive the fastest mail coach on the Great North Road seemed to her to be very exciting and romantic. She was willing to overlook the difference in their ages and the fact that he was quite an ordinary-looking man. In fact, aside from his great skill as a driver, Tom Driffield was just what he looked like, a very ordinary man. But Nance did not see this at first, and she agreed to marry him.

Their intention to marry was to be announced on the last Sunday in April in the church in the village of Sheriff Hutton where Nance lived. Driffield himself could not be in church that day, as he had to make one of his regular runs on the Great North Road.

Normally, the only ones to attend church at Sheriff Hutton were villagers, people Nance had known all her life. But on this particular day there was a stranger in the church. He was a young, slender, and elegant-looking man. Though no one knew who he was, the stranger was immediately taken to one of the pews reserved for members of the gentry. The usher in the church simply assumed that so richly dressed a figure could not possibly be a commoner.

From the moment Nance caught sight of the stranger, she could not take her eyes off him. Her sister, Prue, even scolded her. "You're staring, Nance. It's not polite."

"Who is he?" whispered Nance.

"Some gentleman down from London," said Prue. "He's been staying at the inn since Thursday."

All through the service Nance kept sneaking glances at the handsome stranger. And—was it only her imagination?—he seemed to be looking over at her.

After the service, many of the villagers gathered around Nance outside of the church to congratulate her on her upcoming marriage. But Nance barely heard them. She kept looking over at the church door, waiting for the stranger to come out. And he did. But instead of walking off toward the inn, as might be expected, he walked directly toward Nance.

Removing his hat, he said, "Ma'am, I believe I have the honor and pleasure of addressing the young lady whose marriage was announced this morning."

Nance was so embarrassed that she could barely answer.

"Ma'am," he said, "may a stranger offer one of the prettiest girls he has ever seen his most cordial wishes. Your future husband is the most fortunate of men."

Though it was not immediately obvious to the friends and neighbors who stood around Nance that April morning, her life had been changed forever. Next to this radiant stranger, Tom Driffield, the coachman, seemed unbearably old and dull.

Three days later, the village of Sheriff Hutton was alive with gossip. Nance had run off with the stranger. She left a note for her parents and one for Tom Driffield. She begged his forgiveness, though she did not expect it.

Driffield accepted the news calmly. He went back to driving his coach, and never said a word against Nance. In December, he married a girl from the village of Trask.

No one heard anything of Nance. It was as if she had dropped off the face of the earth.

On a miserably rainy day in March of the following year, Driffield was driving his coach south and was a few miles from York, when he saw a woman with an infant in her arms standing by the side of the road. Though she looked as if she had aged twenty years in under a year, Driffield immediately recognized Nance, and reined his horses to a stop.

Both Nance and her child were obviously very ill. She was so weak that she could only whisper the words "Dear Tom." Driffield took them to York, where he found a room for the sick woman and her child, and brought a doctor to see them. The doctor's report was grim. He did not believe that either Nance or her child could survive for long.

That night Driffield sat by Nance's bedside. He asked no questions, and never complained about having been betrayed. Nance, however, wanted to tell her story. It was a sad and terrible one. The handsome stranger turned out to be a highwayman—a robber. After going through a marriage ceremony, and finding herself pregnant, she discovered that he was already married, and he soon abandoned her. She had worked as a servant for a while, but when the baby was born she was turned out, and had wandered the countryside until Driffield found her alongside the road.

Driffield left Nance in the care of the landlady, and

promised to return on his next trip north. When he did, he was told that both Nance and the baby had already died.

The landlady told Driffield that before Nance died, she said, "Dear Tom, he never uttered a word of reproach. Tell him that to repay his kindness, I will come back to help him." And the landlady added, "She'll keep her promise. You see if her words don't come true."

Nothing unusual happened for two years. Then one day, Driffield was given a special commission. He was to pick up four very important passengers in Durham and drive them to York. The passengers were extremely anxious to get to their destination as quickly as possible. They offered Driffield five times the usual fare if they could arrive in York by eight in the evening.

It would be a near thing, and no other driver could accomplish the feat, but Driffield felt that if the weather held he might just be able to make the trip in time. All went well until about six-thirty, when the coach was seven miles from York and ran into a thick fog.

Driffield told his passengers that unless the fog cleared quickly, it would be impossible to reach York by eight. The passengers insisted that their trip was a matter of life and death, and offered to double the amount of money they had already promised.

"It's not a matter of money," said Driffield. "Driving in heavy fog is dangerous, and it wouldn't do much good if we were killed. Still, if you say it is urgent, I will try."

When Driffield climbed back up into the coachman's box, he found another figure already there. It was Nance, and she had the horses' reins in her hands. She shook them and the horses took off at a gallop.

For seven miles they raced wildly through the swirling fog. The passengers inside the coach were groaning and crying out in alarm, but Driffield had absolute faith in the coach's driver. He was sure Nance would keep her promise. And so she did. The coach arrived at its destination at five minutes to eight.

The passengers were almost speechless with fright. Finally, one of them said, "We never thought that you would drive through such thick fog at breakneck speed. I'll wager no other gentlemen in England have ever had such an experience."

Driffield laughed. "No other gentlemen in England have ever had such a coachman."

That was the first of many appearances that Nance made to Driffield. When he retired, and turned the coaching business over to his son, he told him the story of Nance, and said that he was sure she would come to his aid as well.

There is no record that Nance ever appeared to Driffield's son, but his grandson reported how the ghost had once saved him from a group of highwaymen, by standing in the road and alerting him to the planned ambush.

The Great North Road, which was once used by horsemen and coaches, has been turned into a major highway for automobiles. But even today, from time to time, drivers report that they had been warned of possible danger, or otherwise helped by the appearance of a young woman wearing eighteenth-century clothes. Tom Driffield's act of kindness seems to have survived the centuries.

10

Deadly Crossings

In 1978, a Mr. and Mrs. Hewitt were taking a scenic drive around the English countryside one Sunday afternoon. They were unfamiliar with the area and checked their map frequently. They saw that the road they were on had to pass over a railway line at a spot called Utterby Halt.

The Hewitts didn't know how frequently trains ran on the line, and there were no signals or gates at the crossing, so they approached very cautiously. But as soon as their car moved onto the tracks it stopped dead, for no apparent reason. In spite of all he could do, Mr. Hewitt was unable to restart the engine. The Hewitts suddenly began to feel frightened and feared that a train might come along and hit their car.

They decided to get out of the car and off the track.

But before they were able to do this, their car was hit by a violent gust of wind, which shook the vehicle, and there was a loud roaring sound like that of an oncoming train. The combination of wind and sound so terrified the couple that they were virtually paralyzed. They were sure that a train was heading right for them.

The whole incident lasted less than a minute. It was followed by an eerie silence, and when Mr. Hewitt tried to restart the car, the engine turned over immediately. They drove a short way, stopped, and went back to look at the track. It was rusty, and choked with weeds. The line had obviously been abandoned for some time. They could find nothing to account for their strange experience, for the weather had been perfectly calm before they reached the track.

Their story came to the attention of W. B. Herbert, a writer with an interest in the mysterious and unexplained. After some research, he discovered that in 1953, before the line was abandoned, a railway worker named Lancaster had accidentally stepped out in front of a fast-moving freight train at Utterby Halt, during a dense fog. Lancaster was killed instantly. Further research indicated that a woman had been killed in a similar accident during the 1920s, and that there had been several other serious, but nonfatal, accidents at the crossing.

Did these accidents of the past have anything to do with the Hewitts' strange experience? No one knows.

*   *   *

A railroad crossing at a place called Conington had a reputation for narrow escapes, and deadly accidents. The worst took place on March 1, 1948. World War II had not been over for too long, and there still were German prisoners-of-war in England. Six of them were killed and five more injured, when the truck in which they were riding was hit by a train while crossing the track of the Peterborough-London line in a dense fog.

It was not that accident, but one which took place later that same year that triggered the ghostly appearances.

The crossing was on a narrow road. There were gates which blocked the tracks. It was up to the driver to get out of his car, look up and down the line to see if there was a train coming. If all was clear, then the driver opened the gates, got back into his car and drove across the tracks. It was a cumbersome procedure, but a common one at isolated crossings during that time. There were all sorts of warning notices posted near the crossing, but inevitably some people got careless.

On October 16, 1948, at about 5:30 P.M., Col. A.H. Mellows and his friend A.F. Percival were returning home from a day's hunting near Conington. They were riding in the colonel's large black Chrysler, accompanied by his favorite dog, a Labrador retriever. When they reached the crossing, both men got out of the car. The colonel looked up and down the line, and seeing nothing, told Percival to open the gates. He went back to the car and drove onto the track. He never noticed the high-speed express that came bearing down on him. The train ploughed into the car and instantly killed the colonel and his dog.

Colonel Mellows was given a funeral with full honors. His dog was buried near the spot where the accident took place.

Since that time a lot of people, particularly railroad workers, have had strange experiences at the crossing. The crossing gate would often be found swinging open mysteriously, after it had been securely locked. Several railroad men reported seeing a large black car draw up to the crossing, obviously waiting to cross the track. Before they had a chance to walk down to the road, the car vanished. It did not cross the track; it simply disappeared. Some reported that they saw this car clearly enough to make out the hood ornament, the figure of a winged lady, the Chrysler hood ornament. Those who did not actually see the car said they heard the crunch of gravel, as an invisible car approached the tracks. At least half a dozen men simply refused to work at that particular location.

Others took the strange occurrences in stride. Norman Jinks worked at the crossing for years. He used to walk his dog near the tracks, but whenever the animal passed the spot where Colonel Mellows's Labrador was buried, it became very excited and tried to run away.

Even today, when the crossing has been modernized and completely changed, local people still regard the spot with some fear.

In 1935, Tom Ackroyd was put in charge of a signal box at a remote station called Entwhistle Halt. He controlled the gates that allowed farmers' carts to cross the tracks. There was an occasional, very occasional, passenger at the station. The main business for the trains that stopped at Entwhistle Halt was to pick up milk. Ackroyd, a bachelor, lived in a small house near the station.

One day he looked out the window of his signal box and saw a boy of about eight or nine running through the fields near the track. He knew most of the local people, but did not recognize the boy. Still, he thought nothing of it, because the boy seemed to be behaving in a perfectly normal way. The boy appeared every weekend throughout the summer. He was a thin, pale lad, and Ackroyd suspected that he might be recovering from an illness.

After September, the boy did not come back to the fields. Since the weather usually began to turn cold in September, Ackroyd was not surprised. The boy was back the following spring. As usual, he played in the fields, but he seemed to be coming ever closer to the

tracks. A couple of times, Ackroyd saw him standing right up against the crossing gates, his face almost pressing up against the bars. Ackroyd thought he looked pathetic. He stood by the gates every evening, and was always gone before the 5:13 train to Blackburn went through. This went on for several years. By that time, Britain was fighting World War II, and Ackroyd had a lot more on his mind than a strange boy standing by the tracks.

One Saturday, late in June, in the last year of the war, Ackroyd had just passed the 5:13 through as usual, when there was a commotion up the line. A short time later, he learned that a farmer by the name of Bill Oldenshaw had fallen under the train at the crossing and was killed.

The foreman of the line came to Ackroyd and said, "This is a bad business. That's the second member of the Oldenshaw family that has gone the same way."

"No," said Ackroyd. "I've been here for years, and it's never happened before."

"It happened well before your time," said the foreman. "Bill was no more than a baby, when his brother Harold, who was about eight or nine at the time, was killed at the crossing. Harold was always running and playing in that field out there."

Suddenly, Ackroyd felt a chill.

The foreman continued. "The lad used to look out for his dad's cart in the evening. One evening his dad was late. Harold just stood with his face up against the gate, waiting. Then he must have seen his father and the cart, because the next thing anyone knew, he went right through the gate and across the track and right under the wheels of the 5:29. Now Bill has been hit by a train. It's a bad business."

Ackroyd agreed, but said no more.

11

The Death Car

When Vince Gregory saw the ad in the newspaper, he couldn't believe it. A 1987 Jaguar for $1,000. Vince had always wanted a Jaguar. And he could handle the $1,000, but the price was so ridiculously low that he assumed the ad was a misprint. Still, on a lark, he decided to go and check out the dealer.

The address in the ad led Vince to a perfectly ordinary-looking used car lot. The salesman was a fat, jolly fellow who kept mopping his sweaty forehead with a handkerchief.

"I've come about the Jaguar," said Vince. "I suppose the ad was a misprint and you're selling it for $10,000."

"Nope," said the fat salesman. "The price is correct, $1,000."

"Oh, I see," said Vince. "This is one of those bait-

and-switch deals. You're going to tell me you just sold the Jag, but can offer me something nearly as good, and just a little more expensive, right?"

The salesman kept right on smiling. "Nobody's bought it yet. Car's right over there." He waved his hand toward the far end of the lot where a gorgeous maroon Jaguar was parked.

"This is a joke. You're going to tell me the car hasn't got an engine in it or something, isn't that it?" said Vince.

"Runs real good," said the salesman. He dangled a set of keys in front of Vince's face. "See for yourself; take it out for a test drive."

Vince approached the car reverently. He ran his hands over the real leather upholstery and gently caressed the wooden paneling on the dashboard. When he turned the key, the hum of the engine made him shiver with delight. This was the car of his dreams.

The salesman was right; the Jaguar ran beautifully. The only slightly discordant note was that he detected a faintly unpleasant odor in the car. Vince put the odor down to the leather upholstery. He had never even ridden in a car with leather upholstery before, and didn't know what it was supposed to smell like. "I'll get used to it," he thought.

As Vince headed back to the lot, he began to fear that when he got there the fat salesman would be gone, and a new man who wouldn't sell the car would have taken over. But the fat guy was still there, smiling away.

"I've got my checkbook," said Vince, "but I suppose you'll want me to go to the bank and get a certified check or something."

"Not necessary," grinned the salesman. "I've got all the paperwork ready for you. Just make out the check and drive away."

The salesman looked so happy when Vince pulled out of the lot in the shiny, $1,000 Jag that Vince couldn't shake the feeling that the guy had just put something over on him. But he couldn't figure out what.

When Vince's wife, Candy, saw the car, she hit the roof. "Have you gone crazy? We can't afford a car like that."

When he told her it only cost $1,000, she didn't believe him. He showed her the bill of sale, and she still didn't believe him. But after about an hour, he convinced her to at least take a ride in the Jaguar. That did it! Not only did the car run like a dream, all the neighbors came out to stare in envy. Candy decided she loved the car.

Over the next couple of weeks, Vince and Candy took a lot of rides in the Jag, and while they were together it was great. But when Vince took the car alone, he noticed that smell again. And every time he took it out alone, the smell got a little worse. It went from mildly annoying to absolutely overpowering. Vince tried everything. He rode with the windows wide open, and with the windows shut tight with the air conditioning going full blast. He scrubbed the inside of the car with every imaginable kind of cleaner. He had the car profession- ally cleaned, inside and out, three times. The guys at the car wash thought he was nuts. Nothing helped. The smell got so bad that Vince felt as if he was going to throw up when he drove.

And it wasn't just the smell. When Vince looked into the rearview mirror, he sometimes saw the foggy outline of a man sitting in the backseat. When he turned around, no one was there. As time went on, the form became clearer. It was a man all right, with a heavy- featured, brutal face. The face seemed to be sneering at him.

Vince began to fear that he was losing his mind. But everything was fine, so long as he didn't drive the Jaguar alone. So he began leaving it at home. He told Candy she should have a chance to drive it. At first, Candy was delighted, but then Vince began to notice that the car spent more and more time just sitting in the driveway.

From the time they had first met, Vince and Candy had always talked freely to one another. There had been no secrets between them. But now it seemed as if some- thing had come up between them, something they could not talk about.

They were sitting morosely at breakfast one morning, when Vince finally said, "Listen, about the car. Maybe

I'm going crazy, but I think there's something wrong."

"You, too?" said Candy. "Thank goodness! I thought it was just me."

"The horrible smell," said Vince.

"Yes."

"And that awful face in the mirror."

"Yes, and it's getting worse."

"We've got to take the car back," said Vince.

"Of course we do," said Candy.

The very next day they drove the Jaguar to the used car lot. The fat salesman was standing out front, smiling. It was almost as if he had been expecting them.

"You've come back," he said. "They always come back. That's why the car is so cheap."

"What's wrong with it?" asked Vince.

"I don't really know," said the salesman. "I only know what I've been told. The car used to belong to Maxie Norman, a big-time gangster. Some of Maxie's associates thought he was double-crossing them, so they shot him, stuffed his body in the trunk of his Jaguar, and left it in the airport parking lot. The car was parked there for over a month in the middle of summer before anybody checked it. By that time, you can imagine that Maxie's corpse was pretty ripe. It was the smell that first tipped the cops off that something was wrong. Anyway, they cleaned the car up, and sold it at a police auction. Trouble was that people who bought it brought it back because they said it still had the smell of death

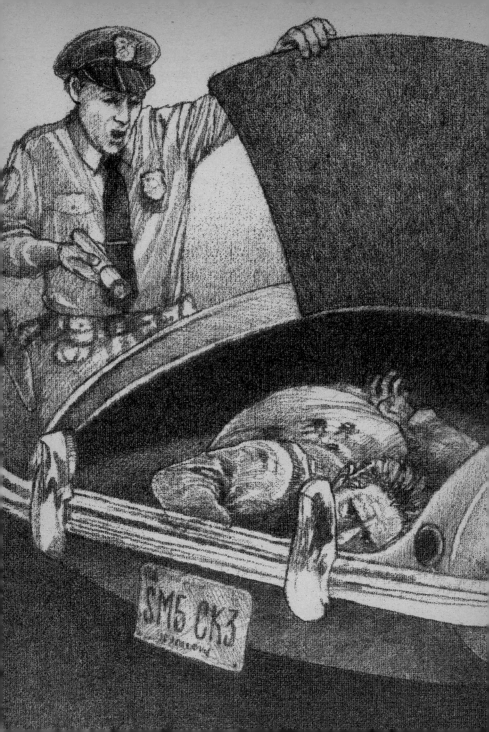

in it, and that the smell was getting stronger day by day. That's what people who have owned the car always say.

"And then there's the face. You saw that, too, I guess. People who have seen pictures of Maxie Norman say it looks just like him."

12

Open 24 Hours

Bill McCormick knew he still had a long way to drive, but he was getting very, very, sleepy. He was actually beginning to doze off at the wheel, and that, as Bill knew very well, could be extremely dangerous. He wasn't even sure exactly where he was anymore, a sign that he had been dozing, for Bill was normally a very careful and attentive driver.

"What I need," Bill thought, "is a good strong cup of black coffee. Maybe even two cups."

But Bill was driving down a dark and deserted two-lane road. He couldn't even see any houses. He had passed through a little town just a few miles back. But the whole place was dark. Nothing was open.

"Where am I going to get coffee out here in the middle of nowhere at this time of night?"

Bill tried singing, even slapping his own face, to stay awake. It was a losing battle. If he kept on driving in this condition, he was going to fall asleep at the wheel and wind up in a ditch, or worse. Bill began to look for a place where he could pull off to the side of the road and take a nap. He didn't like to sleep in his car, particularly on a deserted road. You never can tell what might happen. Now he didn't feel he had any choice.

Then, as he came around a curve, he saw a green and red flashing neon sign, DINER OPEN 24 HOURS. "Saved!" he thought. Here, at last he could get that coffee. He wouldn't have to sleep in the car.

The place was a small, old-fashioned type of roadside diner. It was all aluminum, and built to look like a railroad car. There had been thousands of diners like this all across America in the late 1940s and early '50s. Now they had been pretty much replaced by fast food outlets. No great loss, thought Bill. Diner food was generally pretty awful. Bill pulled into the parking lot. There was only one other car there, parked over to the side. Bill couldn't see the car too clearly. It looked old, about the same vintage as the diner itself. Bill figured it must belong to the owner.

"I wonder how a place like this manages to stay in business," he thought. "There can't be much traffic on this road, particularly at night."

The interior of the diner was every bit as dreary as Bill feared it would be. It wasn't anything he could really put his finger on. The place looked clean enough, but everything seemd shabby, worn, and patched together. The Formica counter was chipped and cracked. The vinyl seats had been repaired with tape. Even the old-fashioned sugar pourer was missing the little metal flap that covered the spout. There were a couple of very tired-looking pieces of pie, flavor unknown, on display under a clear plastic cover. They looked so ancient and unappetizing that Bill decided that he would take only coffee.

Bill sat down, and glanced over at the surly looking young man behind the counter. He was about twenty, and wore his abundant dark hair well greased, and combed back. Bill expected him to come over and take his order, but the young man looked away and didn't move.

"Why don't you wait on the customers?" growled a thin, elderly man who was cleaning the grill. "You gotta give people service, or they won't come back."

"Customers," muttered the young man. "One guy comes in and we got customers." Still, he walked over to Bill, looked at him, and asked what he wanted.

"I'll just have a cup of coffee," Bill said, "black."

"You see, the guy only wants coffee," said the young man loudly.

He went over to the coffee urn, hastily filled a mug and slapped it down on the counter in front of Bill, spilling half of it. A care-worn-looking, gray-haired woman with a rag in her hand appeared. Bill didn't know where she had come from. She began frantically to wipe up the counter in front of him, and she refilled the mug.

"You want some cream for that?" she asked.

"No, this is fine."

"How about some pie?" she said. "We have very nice pie." The gray-haired woman pointed to the dried-out pieces beneath the plastic cover.

"No, please, I'm fine."

The woman kept wiping the counter, even though it was by now quite clean. "Don't take him to heart," she whispered, motioning toward the young man. "He's a good boy. He's just been working too hard." The greasy-haired young man heard what she said and snorted. The older man kept relentlessly cleaning the grill.

There was such an air of tension, even desperation, about the place that Bill really wanted to just leave his coffee and get back to his car. But he was afraid that might provoke something. So he drank it down. It was awful, as he had expected. It tasted as if it had been sitting in the urn for a long time. He declined the gray-haired woman's urgings of a second cup. He just paid for the coffee, which seemed amazingly cheap, though considering the quality, perhaps still overpriced.

It was with a real sigh of relief that he left the place and got back into his car. The experience, as much as the coffee, had left him wide awake. He wasn't worried about falling asleep at the wheel anymore.

As he pulled out of the parking lot, he saw the gray-haired woman in the doorway of the diner, waving at him. He wasn't going back there, so he pretended not to notice, and just drove off.

An hour later, a thoroughly exhausted Bill Mc-Cormick reached his destination. As he was undressing for bed, he realized that his wallet was missing. He had taken out his wallet when he paid for his coffee at the diner. "I was in such a hurry to get out of the place I must have left it on the counter," he thought. "Now I'll have to go back there."

The following morning Bill seriously considered just forgetting about the wallet. But he figured that getting a new driver's license and canceling all his credit cards would be more difficult than driving back to the diner.

Bill thought he had a pretty good general idea of where the place was, and he figured it wouldn't be too hard to find because it was probably the only diner on the road. But at first, he wasn't able to locate it. He drove over the same stretch of road where he knew the diner must be four times before he realized what was wrong. The place was there all right, but it was not only closed; it looked as if it had been abandoned for years.

The parking lot was overgrown with weeds. The windows were partially boarded over. The big DINER OPEN 24 HOURS sign had half-fallen down. As Bill drove up, he saw that there was another car in the lot, over to the side, just as there had been last night. But the car was just a rusting hulk, as abandoned as the building it stood next to.

Though Bill was feeling very uneasy, he forced himself to peer into one of the windows where the boards had fallen away. The inside of the diner was as he remembered it, but even older and drearier-looking. Clearly, no one had been inside the place for years. There was a thick layer of dust on everything. As his eyes became accustomed to the gloom, Bill thought he could make out a set of fresh footprints in the dust, from the door to the counter. And over by the cash register he saw something familiar, something that made him sweat and shiver at the same time. It was his wallet.

He went to the police station in the nearest town. Before he told his story to the officer behind the desk, he launched into a long explanation about how crazy the story sounded, but that he was not crazy, nor had he been drinking or anything like that.

Bill wasn't even allowed to finish his explanation. The officer raised his hand and said, "It's about Tom and Edna's diner, about five miles down the road, isn't it?"

"Yes," said Bill, now more puzzled than ever. "I was there last night, and left my wallet. When I went back, the place looked like it had been closed for years. I don't know what happened."

"It's a pretty depressing story," said the officer. "Tom and Edna Porter built the place right after World War

II, put every penny they had into it. They thought that there was going to be an exit from the Interstate that would funnel traffic right by them and that they would do a big business. The exit was never built, and traffic on the road in front of their diner just dried up.

"Tom and Edna couldn't walk away from their dream—they had invested too much of themselves in it—so they kept on working the place with their son, Bert. They believed that if they worked hard enough they would somehow be able to make a go of it. It was impossible, of course; there never was going to be enough traffic to support a diner at that spot. They really did keep it open twenty-four hours a day, just the three of them. No one knows how. The place was usually empty, particularly at night, and they didn't have the money to fix anything.

"The strain got pretty bad. They used to fight all the time, and drive away the few customers they had. For Tom and Edna, the diner had become an obsession. They couldn't stop, even though it was hopeless, and was killing them. Bert should have left, but he wasn't the brightest guy in the world. He just hung on unitl one night the strain became too much. There was a big argument and he shot his parents, and himself. That was back in 1956. Murder-suicide makes a big splash in a little town like this. Nobody ever forgot the case. The diner has been boarded-up ever since.

"A lot of people say they have seen lights on in the

102

diner at night. I've never seen them myself, but my wife has. No local person would ever go into the place, though a couple of tourists say that they have. You're the first person who ever left something there.

"I hope you didn't have anything too valuable in that wallet, because I'm not going to get it for you. And I don't think you're going to want to either."

13

Horrible
Happenings

Lisa Gunther was driving down a busy California free-way. In the front seat of her car she had a gerbil in a cage. She had just purchased the furry animal as a pet for her daughter. But Lisa had failed to check and see if the cage was properly locked. It wasn't, and the gerbil escaped. The frightened animal, looking for a place to hide, climbed up Lisa's shoulder and ran down the front of her blouse.

Lisa became nearly hysterical, yet she had the presence of mind to be able to pull over to the side of the road, stop the car, and jump out. She threw herself on the ground near the car and began rolling around and flailing her arms, and screaming, trying to get the animal out of her blouse.

Harry Baxter was driving by and saw Lisa thrashing around on the ground. His first thought was, "That poor lady is having a seizure or something. I have to help her before she hurts herself."

So Harry pulled over, and jumped out of his car. He rushed over to Lisa and tried to pin her shoulders to the ground, in his misguided effort to stop what he thought were convulsions.

Claude Benoit passed the scene and saw what he thought was a man trying to wrestle a screaming and flailing woman to the ground. "Oh, no, that guy's attacking a woman!" he said. Claude also pulled over to the side, jumped out of his car, ran over to Lisa and Harry, and punched Harry in the face, breaking his jaw.

And all of this happened because of an innocent little gerbil.

Mrs. Franklin, who was very rich, was driving her shiny blue Mercedes around a very crowded parking lot. After circling for some twenty minutes, she was getting extremely frustrated and angry. Finally, she spotted another driver getting ready to leave. Mrs. Franklin pulled up alongside and waited. Just as the other car pulled out, a young man in a flashy red sports car zipped into the space Mrs. Franklin had been waiting for.

The driver of the sports car stuck his head out the window, grinned at Mrs. Franklin, and shouted, "You've got to be young and fast."

Mrs. Franklin sat and thought for a moment. Then, very deliberately, she pressed down on the accelerator and rammed the sports car hard. She backed up and did it again and again.

The horrified young man came rushing up to her, shouting, "Are you crazy? What are you doing?"

Mrs. Franklin smiled benignly and said, "You've got to be old and rich." Then she drove calmly away.

Tony Blundell was a truck driver, though he didn't look like one. Tony was a small, mild-looking man with thick glasses and a receding hairline. He didn't in any way resemble the popular image of the big, burly truck driver, but that's just what he was.

One night Tony pulled his rig into a truck stop to have dinner. He had polished off the meatloaf and had just ordered pie and coffee when a pair of tough-looking, tattooed, leather-clad bikers burst in. The bikers were feeling good, and that could be bad news for anyone who happened to be in their way. They looked around the diner for someone to intimidate, and they settled on the weakest-looking guy in the place, Tony.

They took seats at the counter next to Tony, and began talking loudly, insulting his size, his glasses, and his baldness. Tony said nothing.

When Tony's pie and coffee arrived, one of the bikers grabbed the pie and ate it. The other drank his coffee. Still, Tony said nothing. He just got up, paid his bill, including the pie he never ate and the coffee he never drank, and left the diner.

The bikers had a big laugh over this. "He's not much of a man," one of them said.

The sound of Tony's truck could be heard pulling out of the parking lot. The cashier looked out the window and said, "He's not much of a driver either. He just ran over a couple of motorcycles as he was pulling out."

Have you ever driven behind a truck heavily laden with some heavy and dangerous-looking cargo, and wondered what would happen if a piece of that cargo fell off? Of course you have; everybody has. Then this gory little account that comes from England will give you a shudder.

A big truck loaded with thin sheets of steel was making its way slowly along a highway in the industrial part of the Midlands. A man on a motorcycle with a sidecar came up behind the truck. The motorcyclist wanted to get ahead of the slow-moving truck, so he pulled up close to it, and tried to look around it for oncoming traffic. Seeing no traffic, he prepared to pass. Just when the motorcyclist was even with the truck, the top sheet of steel, which had not been firmly tied down, slid loose and flew off the truck, right toward the cyclist.

The sheet of metal was like the blade of a guillotine; it cleanly sliced the head off the cyclist. But the headless corpse's hands still convulsively gripped the throttle, and the sidecar kept the motorcycle upright. As a result, the cycle kept gaining on the truck, and eventually passed it.

The truck driver looked out of his window and saw his truck being passed by a headless cyclist. The sight so shocked him that he had a heart attack. The out-of-control truck lurched across the highway right into a group of people who were waiting for a bus.

The result was one of the worst highway accidents in British history.

Finally, there is the tale of Larry Holland, who was driving down the street, minding his own business, when a car that had just come around the corner, passed him from the opposite direction.

The woman who was driving the car, stuck her head out the window, and shouted, "Pig!"

Startled and insulted, Larry shouted back, "You're not so good-looking yourself!"

He then turned the corner and ran smack into a pig that had escaped from a truck and was standing in the middle of the street.

Daniel Cohen has written many books on many subjects, ranging from science to the supernatural. He is considered an authority on monsters, and knows all about ghosts. His book titles include *Great Ghosts*, *America's Very Own Ghosts*, *Real Ghosts*, *The World's Most Famous Ghosts*, *Phone Call from a Ghost*.

Mr. Cohen is former managing editor of *Science Digest* magazine. He and his wife, Susan, have collaborated on a number of books and recently did *What Kind of Dog Is That?: Rare and Unusual Breeds of Dogs*. They live in Port Jervis, New York.

Stephen Marchesi, a graduate of Pratt Institute, is a well-known illustrator of book jackets and of three picture books for children. He tried to capture in these illustrations for *Railway Ghosts and Highway Horrors* the eeriness of a dark night and the sudden flash of terror.

Mr. Marchesi and his wife live in Peekskill, New York.

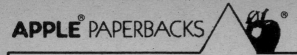

APPLE® PAPERBACKS

Pick an Apple and Polish Off Some Great Reading!

BEST-SELLING APPLE TITLES

- ❏ MT43944-8 **Afternoon of the Elves** Janet Taylor Lisle — $2.75
- ☑ MT43109-9 **Boys Are Yucko** Anna Grossnickle Hines — $2.75
- ❏ MT43473-X **The Broccoli Tapes** Jan Slepian — $2.95
- ❏ MT42709-1 **Christina's Ghost** Betty Ren Wright — $2.75
- ❏ MT43461-6 **The Dollhouse Murders** Betty Ren Wright — $2.75
- ❏ MT43444-6 **Ghosts Beneath Our Feet** Betty Ren Wright — $2.75
- ❏ MT44351-8 **Help! I'm a Prisoner in the Library** Eth Clifford — $2.75
- ❏ MT44567-7 **Leah's Song** Eth Clifford — $2.75
- ❏ MT43618-X **Me and Katie (The Pest)** Ann M. Martin — $2.75
- ❏ MT41529-8 **My Sister, The Creep** Candice F. Ransom — $2.75
- ❏ MT42883-7 **Sixth Grade Can Really Kill You** Barthe DeClements — $2.75
- ❏ MT40409-1 **Sixth Grade Secrets** Louis Sachar — $2.75
- ❏ MT42882-9 **Sixth Grade Sleepover** Eve Bunting — $2.75
- ❏ MT41732-0 **Too Many Murphys** Colleen O'Shaughnessy McKenna — $2.75

Available wherever you buy books, or use this order form.

Scholastic Inc., P.O. Box 7502, 2931 East McCarty Street, Jefferson City, MO 65102

Please send me the books I have checked above. I am enclosing $_____ (please add $2.00 to cover shipping and handling). Send check or money order — no cash or C.O.D.s please.

Name _____

Address _____

City_____ State/Zip _____

Please allow four to six weeks for delivery. Offer good in the U.S.A. only. Sorry, mail orders are not available to residents of Canada. Prices subject to change.

APP591